A goodnight kiss

Written by Jillian Harker

Illustrated by Andrew-Everitt-Stewart

PaRragon

Bath · New York · Singapore · Hong Kong · Cologne · Delhi · Melbourne

"It's bedtime now, Jake," said Mom.

Jake curled up in the chair.
His ears began to droop and he muttered,
"Oh, that's not fair!"

"Have a drink first," smiled Mom, "then you must go."
"Five minutes more!" begged Jake.
Mom answered, "No!"

Jake's ears drooped and off he went.
But he was **back in a flash!**

"Where's your drink?" asked Mom.
"You haven't been very long.
You look scared, Jake.
Is there something wrong?"

"There's a monster
in the kitchen,
with long, white shaggy hair,
lurking in the corner,
behind the rocking chair,"
said Jake.

Mom laughed.
"Oh, Jake, you've made
a mistake.
That's no monster. It's a mop."
And she gave the mop a shake.

Jake's ears drooped
and off he went.
But he was
back in a flash!

"What's the matter?"
asked Mom.

"There's a ghost
in the hallway, hovering around.
Look, there it is floating
just above the ground,"
he wailed.

"Oh, Jake, you've made a mistake.
That's no ghost.
It's just an old coat, hanging on the hook.
Coats don't float!" laughed Mom.

Jake's ears drooped and off
he went.
But he was
back in a flash!

"Why aren't you in bed, Jake?"
asked Mom.

"There's a
great big lump
beneath the sheets.
It's waiting to get me.
I'm scared it's going to pounce.
Please come and see,"
sniffed Jake.

"Oh, Jake, you've made a mistake.
The only thing underneath the sheets,
is your old teddy bear," smiled Mom.

Jake's ears drooped
and he got into bed.
But he didn't
close his eyes.

"Why aren't you asleep?"
asked Mom.

"There are
huge creepy crawlies
underneath my bed.
And I can't get the thought of them
out of my head,"
complained Jake.

"They're just your
slippers, Jake, so
there's no need to hide.
They won't be creeping
anywhere without
your feet inside,"
grinned Mom.
"That's it now, Jake.
Time to say goodnight."

Mom turned and left the
room, switching off
the light.

And then Jake saw it,
standing by the door.
The monster!

It moved across the floor and
walked straight towards him,
with its arms stretched out.
Jake's mouth opened,
but he found he couldn't shout.

The monster leaned over him and Jake closed his eyes. What happened next gave Jake an enormous surprise. The monster picked him up and cuddled him tight. Monsters just don't do that.

This couldn't be right!

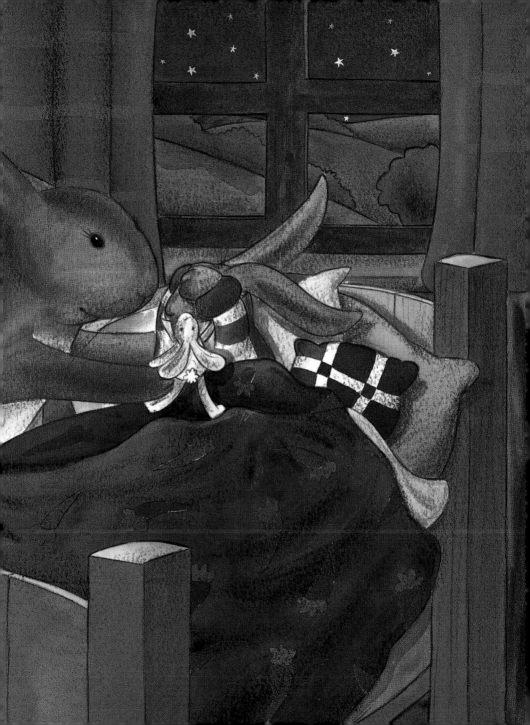

Then Mom's voice whispered
"Don't worry, it's just me.
When I said 'Goodnight' just now,
I forgot to give you this."

Then Monster Mom gave Jake
a goodnight kiss!